Peter Lancett is a writer, edit͏   ͏nd film
maker. He has written m҇   and
has just made a featur͏
Xlitherman.

Peter now lives i͏   and
California.

Dark Man

The Dark Realm of Screams
by Peter Lancett
illustrated by Jan Pedroietta

Published by Ransom Publishing Ltd.
Radley House, 8 St. Cross Road, Winchester, Hampshire
SO23 9HX
www.ransom.co.uk

ISBN   978 184167 989 1

First published in 2010

Copyright © 2010 Ransom Publishing Ltd.

Dark Man

The Dark Realm
of Screams

by Peter Lancett

illustrated by Jan Pedroietta

The Dark Realm of Screams
The Players

 The Dark Man
(138 words)

 Angela
(83 words)

Narrator
(71 words)

 The Old Man
(41 words)

Blind Anna
(39 words)

Insane Man
(18 words)

 Young boy
(15 words)

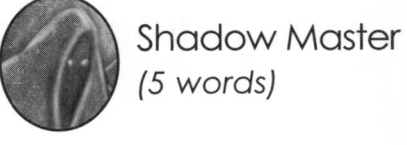 Shadow Master
(5 words)

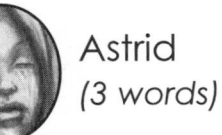 Astrid
(3 words)

The Dark Realm of Screams
The Acts

1

Act One:
The Door

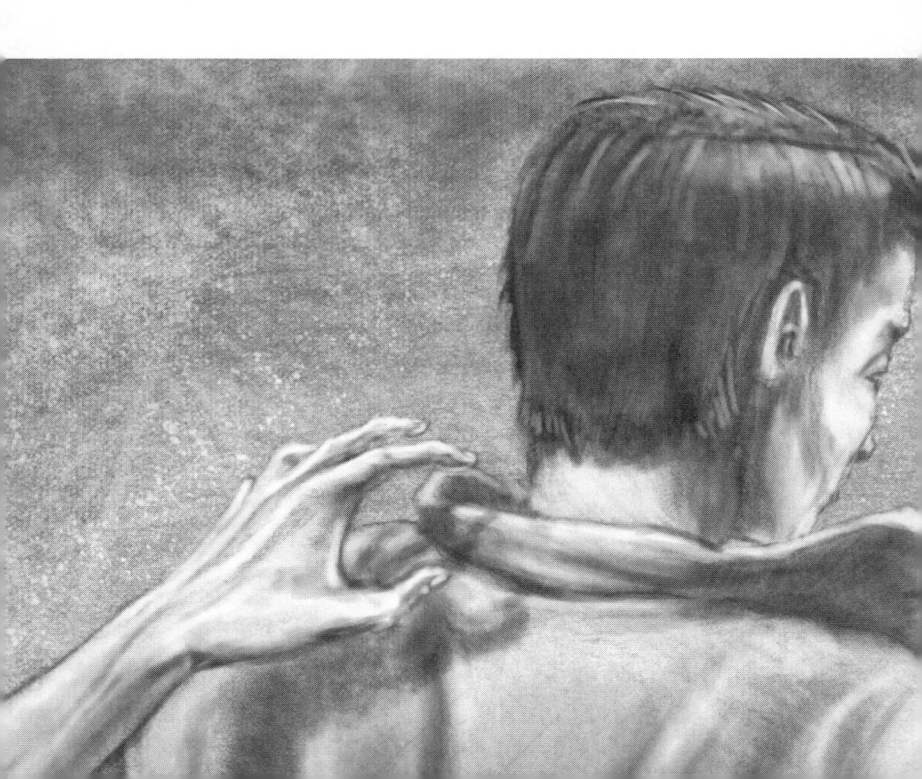

Narrator:
The Old Man creeps up on the Dark Man.

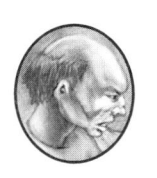

The Old Man:
Put the picture away.
You must forget Astrid
– for now.

 **The Dark Man:**
>   I keep thinking about her.

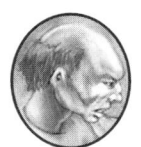

The Old Man:
> But now we have work to
> do. The Shadow Masters
> have opened a door. To
> the Realm of Screams.

The Dark Man:
> We must close it.

The Old Man:
> Yes. But you must find
> Angela. She sees things we
> cannot see.

Narrator:
The Dark Man talks to a young boy.

 **The Dark Man:**
The Old Man says you can
tell me where Angela is.

Young boy:
Angela scares me.

The Dark Man:
You don't have to see her.
Just tell me where she is.

Young boy:
She is in a dark room. Two
floors down from the top.

Act Two:
Angela

Narrator:
> The Dark Man finds Angela. She has been tied up.

The Dark Man:
> Hello Angela. I'd like to say it's good to see you. But it's not.

Angela:
> Shut up and untie me.

The Dark Man:
You have many enemies.

Angela:
You still need me. I bet that
hurts.

The Dark Man:
Just tell me what you have
seen.

Angela:
Just close your eyes. I'll
show you what I've seen.
Unless you're afraid.

The Dark Man:
Afraid of you? Never.

Narrator:
A vision comes to the Dark Man. An insane, screaming man.

Insane man:
Tell them to stop! Tell them to stop! They want to take our skin and eat our brains!

The Dark Man:
I've seen enough. I know what lives in the Realm of Screams.

Angela:
Did you like that? All that pain?

The Dark Man:
Just show me where the gateway is, so that I can close it.

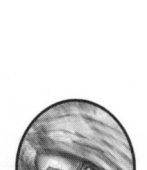

Angela:
I'll take you to Blind Anna. She knows where it is.

3

Act Three:
Blind Anna

Narrator:
> The Dark Man visits Blind
> Anna alone. Angela is
> afraid of her.

The Dark Man:
> You must be Anna.

Blind Anna:
> I know why you are here.
> Come in.

The Dark Man:
Where can I find the
gateway to the Realm of
Screams?

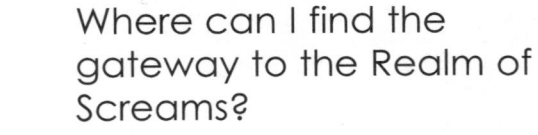

Blind Anna:
> It is a machine, held by a
> little boy.

The Dark Man:
> So I must destroy the
> machine?

Blind Anna:
> No. You must kill the boy.

Narrator:
The Dark Man is leaving.

Blind Anna:
I have sent a vision to Angela. Tell her I will come to find her. Soon.

Act Four:
In the Rain

Narrator:
Outside it is raining.

The Dark Man:
Anna sent you a vision, showing where the gateway is.

Angela:
> She also sent another vision. Want to see it? There is a girl in it.

The Dark Man:
> Show me.

Narrator:
A vision of Astrid comes to the Dark Man.

Astrid:
Help me, David.

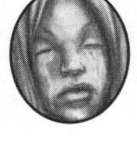

Shadow Master:
You are beyond help now.

Narrator:
The vision ends.

Angela:
I can kill the little boy for you. If you want to save that girl.

The Dark Man:
   You are truly evil.

Angela:
   You love me really.

The Dark Man:
I'll do what I have to do.
Then I'll come back to
deal with you.

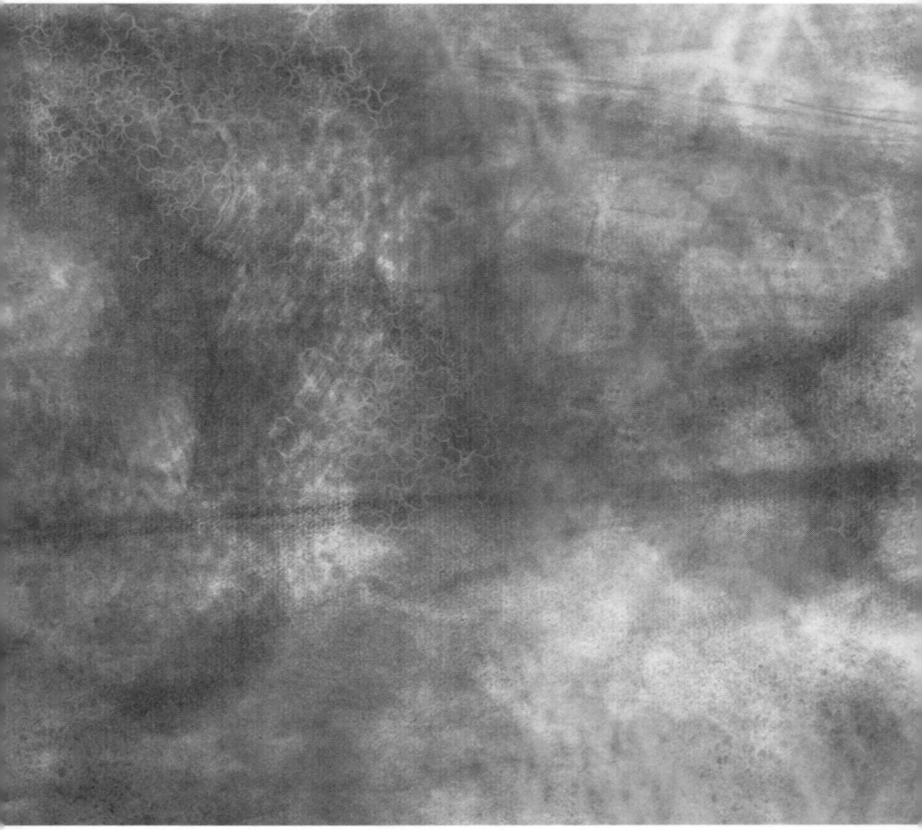

Angela:
I'll look forward to that.

More **Dark Man** books:

Stories

Plays